THIS BOOK
BELONGS TO:

_____

DREAD CAT

AN OLD TALE

MICHAEL ROSEN

DREAD CAT

AN OLD TALE

WITH ILLUSTRATIONS BY

NICOLA O'BYRNE

Barrington Stoke

First published in 2017 in Great Britain by
Barrington Stoke Ltd
18 Walker Street, Edinburgh, EH3 7LP

www.barringtonstoke.co.uk

Text © 2017 Michael Rosen
Illustrations © 2017 Nicola O'Byrne

The moral right of Michael Rosen and Nicola O'Byrne to be
identified as the author and illustrator of this work has been
asserted in accordance with the Copyright, Designs and
Patents Act, 1988

All rights reserved. No part of this publication may be
reproduced in whole or in any part in any form without the
written permission of the publisher

A CIP catalogue record for this book is available
from the British Library upon request

ISBN: 978-1-78112-588-5

Printed in China by Leo

This book is in a super readable format for young readers
beginning their independent reading journey.

For Emma, Elsie and Emile

Contents

CHAPTER 1

THE DREADED
DREAD CAT

Once there was a very fierce cat.

Not just fierce. Well fierce, totally fierce, terrifyingly fierce, stupendously fierce, stinkingly fierce.

Everyone was afraid of this cat.

Its name was Dread. Dread Cat.

Everyone dreaded Dread Cat.

In fact, everyone dreaded Dread Cat so so so so much that all Dread Cat needed to do was turn up and everyone fled.

Whoosh!

Everyone scarpered.

Everyone skedaddled.

Everyone scooted.

So Dread Cat wasn't too good at the mouse-catching business. And, remember, it's the business of cats like Dread Cat to catch mice. It's their job.

And the truth is, Dread Cat wasn't doing his job.

Bad news, huh?

CHAPTER 2
EEEK, EEEK, EEEK

So, Dread Cat had a plan. And Dread Cat told his plan to anyone near or far who could hear his plan.

Listen to how it goes.

"I am giving up chasing mice," Dread Cat said in a very loud voice. "I will never try to catch or kill another mouse. Heaven forbid. The war is over. The war between cat and mouse is over at last. Yes, I said, 'over'. Over-a-diddly-over. And I shall prove it."

Then Dread Cat said, "I invite all of you, all the mice in this house, to come out every night and walk in a long line past me. I will have a piece of cheese ready for you. And when I say 'you', I mean each and every single one of you. You mice will see how I keep my word, oh yes. I will not touch a hair on your head. Not a single mouse. Not a single head. Not a single hair. How about that?"

While Dread Cat spoke, the mice were hiding in their hidey-holes, hunkering down in their tiny homes, cowering under the floorboards as they listened.

Could they believe him?

Should they believe him?

Had Dread Cat really, really, really ended the War Between Cat and Mouse?

Was that possible?

The mice talked and whispered among themselves.

"Pssst, eeek, eeek, pssst, eeek," they said.

Not many people know mouse language, but believe me, this was all about whether they should trust Dread Cat.

In the end, the mice agreed. They would give it a try, and come out for the cheese that Dread Cat put out for them … When you are a mouse, you don't miss the chance of some cheese when someone offers it to you, even if it is Dread Cat doing the offering.

CHAPTER 3

QUICK AS A FLASH

That night Dread Cat sat with his back to the fire, and sorted out a bit of cheese for every mouse in the house. He laid the bits of cheese all out, sat behind them and waited. Waited for the mice.

One by one the mice came out from their hidey-holes and tiny homes. They crept out towards the bits of cheese, grabbed a bit and whooshed back home. And all the while, Dread Cat smiled and purred at each one of them.

In reply, each mouse said, "Thank you, sir," or "Thank you, Dread Cat."

The War Between Cat and Mouse was over.

It was the End of the War.

It was Peace in Our Time.

One by one, the mice came out, took a piece of cheese and – WHOOSH! Off they went home. On they went until the 30th mouse had taken a bit. And then ... on they went until the 40th mouse had taken a bit. And then ... till the 49th mouse had taken a bit.

And then ...

But then ....

Ah, but then ...

The 50th mouse, the very last mouse, the mouse on the end of the line, walked past Dread Cat. Dread Cat's right paw shot out – and quick as you like, quick as a flash, Dread Cat grabbed that 50th mouse and held it tight.

Did any mouse see that?

No. Not at all. All the mice were gone. Even the 49th mouse had slipped down the hole in the wall. The 50th mouse was on its own. Dread Cat didn't waste any time.

GULP!!!!!!

In went the 50th mouse into Dread Cat's mouth. Down went the 50th mouse into Dread Cat's belly. Gone. Just like that.

CHAPTER 4
OVER-A-DIDDLY-OVER

The next night, Dread Cat spoke again.

"Tonight, my friends, it shall be the same. The cheese bits will be ready and waiting for you. You will see that I am as good as my word. I have changed my ways. I do not chase mice. The War Between the Cat and the Mouse is over! Over-a-diddly-over!"

So, that night, one by one, out came 49 mice, in single file out of their hidey-holes, out of their tiny homes …

They filed past Dread Cat, took their bit of cheese, said, "Thank you, sir," and "Thank you, Dread Cat," and then headed off home.

Then, just like the night before, just
as the 49th mouse walked past, Dread
Cat grabbed that 49th mouse off the end
of the line and held it tight.

Did any mouse see that?

No. Not at all.

All the mice were gone. Even the
48th mouse had slipped back down the
hidey-hole in the wall. The 49th mouse
was on its own.

Dread Cat didn't waste any time.

GULP!!!!!!

In went the 49th mouse into Dread Cat's mouth. Down went the 49th mouse into Dread Cat's belly. Gone. Just like that.

And so it went on. Night after night, Dread Cat gobbled up the last mouse on the line.

Well, when a fortnight had gone – that's fourteen days – the number of mice in the house was down to 36.

One of the mice said, "Psst, psst, eek, eek," which means, "Hey, I think there are fewer of us about these days. I mean, I'm sure there was one of us over there under the washing machine. Wasn't there one of us in the cupboard?"

And one of the other mice agreed. "Yes, funny that," it said. "I was thinking the same myself. Yes. We're disappearing."

And another mouse poked its nose out, and that mouse said, "Very, very strange ... but it can't be like the way it used to be ... you know, when Dread Cat used to chase us. It can't be Dread Cat taking us because we all

know that Dread Cat doesn't chase mice. The War Between the Cat and the Mouse is over, over-a-diddly-over."

"Yes ... that's right, it can't be Dread Cat," the other mice agreed.

But one mouse among them wasn't so sure.

"Hey now, folks, hold it there," she said. "I've never heard of a cat that can give up chasing mice once and for ever. Maybe for a while, it can. Maybe when the humans dish out so much cat food that the cat doesn't come bothering us ... but not once and for ever. That doesn't sound right to me."

So, the mice decided to hold a meeting in an hour's time. A meeting for every single mouse in the house.

They met under the floorboards.

And when they had all gathered together from all the different parts of the house, yes, it did look as if there were fewer of them there.

So, how was it happening?

Quite a few of them agreed that somehow or another Dread Cat was getting the better of them.

But how?

"Has anyone seen Dread Cat chase one of us?" one mouse asked.

No, no one had.

"Has anyone seen Dread Cat moving about near us at any other time other than when we file past him?"

No, no one had.

"Has anyone among us just died in our beds? Got ill? Had to see the doctor?"

No, none of them had.

"Well, then," this mouse said, "somehow or another Dread Cat is getting the better of us. He's getting us when we come for the cheese that he's giving us. We have to find out how."

So, they sat and they thought and thought and thought and thought.

At last one of them said, "I've got it. It's pretty complicated, mind. But listen. Every one of us can see the mouse in front, yes? But ... but ... but ... none of us can see the mouse behind. See what I'm saying here? We can't see the mouse behind."

That mouse stopped to think and then he went on. "So what we do tonight, let's each one of us make totally sure that there's not only a mouse in front of us, there's also a mouse behind. You get me?"

Yes, yes, they all understood.

Chapter 6
Are You There?

That night, like all the other nights, the mice filed out of their hidey-holes and tiny homes. That night, like all the other nights, each mouse took a bit of cheese and said, "Thank you, sir," or "Thank you, Dread Cat."

But this night, unlike all the other nights, each mouse looked round and said, "Are you there, bruv?" or "Are you there, sis?"

And each mouse in front or behind said, "Yes, I'm here, bruv," or "Yes, I'm here, sis."

No mouse ever lost sight of the mouse in front and no mouse ever lost sight of the mouse behind.

And this night, no one whooshed off back to their hidey-holes and tiny homes. Instead they gathered together on the side of the wall so that they could keep an eye on Dread Cat.

Mouse 33 said, "Thank you, Dread Cat," – and whooshed over to join the others.

"There you are," one of the mice who believed in Dread Cat said. "You see, it's not Dread Cat's fault."

Mouse 34 said, "Thank you, Dread Cat," – and whooshed over to join the others.

"It's looking good," another mouse said.

Mouse 35 said, "Thank you, sir," but just as Mouse 35 was about to join the others, she looked round and said, "Are you there, sis?"

BUT MOUSE 36 WAS GONE!!!

"Help! Help!" Mouse 35 shouted. "She's gone. Mouse 36 is GONE!!!"

CHAPTER 7
NO MORE TRICKS

"Mouse 36 is GONE!!!" Mouse 35 cried again.

And, at that, all the mice came running and rushed towards Dread Cat.

CHA-A-A-A-A-A-A-A-A-A-ARGE!!!!!!!!

Dread Cat was holding Mouse 36.

Dread Cat looked up.

Dread Cat saw 35 mice hurtling towards him.

Dread Cat dropped Mouse 36.

The 35 mice went on hurtling towards Dread Cat, each one ready to bite or nibble a bit of Dread Cat.

Enough was enough! They weren't willing to let Dread Cat go on tricking them any more.

Dread Cat looked at the onrushing mice with horror on his face.

Then, he turned and ran.

Up onto a window sill Dread Cat ran, out the window, across a roof, and he was never seen or heard of ever again.

Ever.

And that was how the mice saved the life of one mouse to save them all.

Our books are tested
for children and young people by
children and young people.

Thanks to everyone who consulted on
a manuscript for their time and effort in
helping us to make our books better
for our readers.